THE TALE OF THE TURNIP

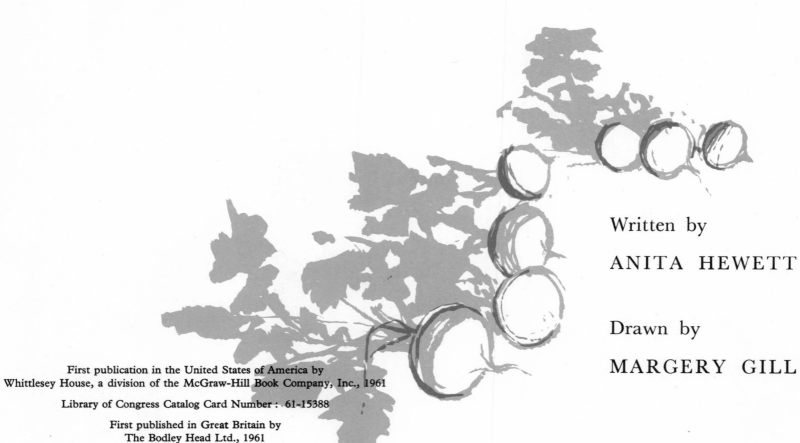

Written by

ANITA HEWETT

Drawn by

MARGERY GILL

First publication in the United States of America by
Whittlesey House, a division of the McGraw-Hill Book Company, Inc., 1961

Library of Congress Catalog Card Number : 61-15388

First published in Great Britain by
The Bodley Head Ltd., 1961

Printed in Great Britain

THE
TALE
OF THE
TURNIP

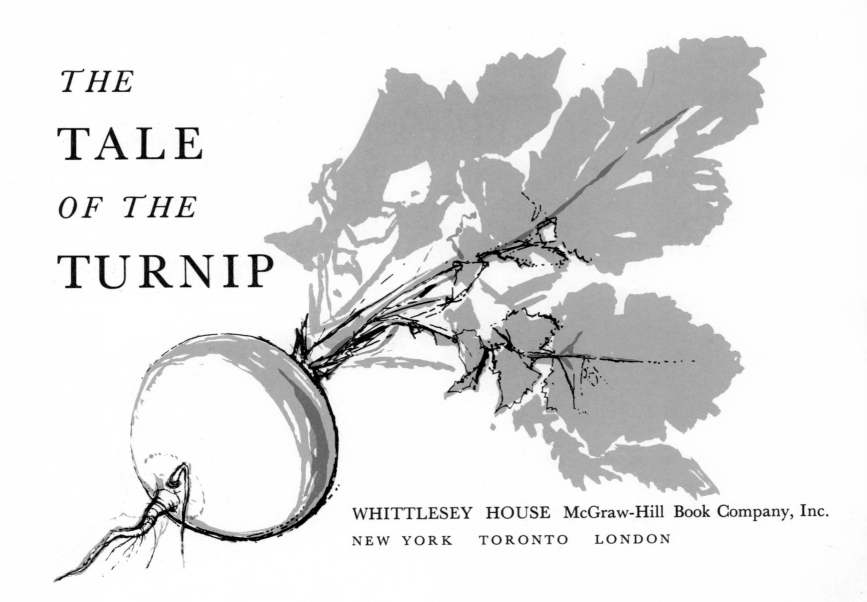

WHITTLESEY HOUSE McGraw-Hill Book Company, Inc.

NEW YORK   TORONTO   LONDON

Once upon a time there was a house on a hill.

It had a red roof, and a green door, and four little windows with yellow curtains.

In front of the house there was a small, neat garden, with a flower bed, a tree, and a vegetable patch.

In the house lived the little old man the grandfather, the little old woman the grandmother, the little girl the grandchild, the little black cat, and the little brown mouse. The little brown mouse had a secret place to live in. *No one* knew where it was, not even the little black cat.

One spring day when the sun was shining,
the little old man the grandfather said : " It is
time to plant my turnip seeds. I shall sow them
now, in the vegetable patch. And when they
have grown to big white turnips, we shall all
have turnip soup for supper."

He opened a drawer
and found the seeds.

He went to the cupboard
for his gardening boots.

8

He went to the garden shed
for his trowel.

And then he went to the vegetable patch.
The earth was dry and hard and lumpy.

The little old man the grandfather dug it up.
He beat out the lumps and smoothed the earth
until he had made a good safe, seed bed.
And then he planted the turnip seeds,
in a long straight row.

" There ! " he said. " That's done."
And he went indoors for his supper.

The rain came and watered the
turnip seeds. The sun shone
and kept them warm.

Beneath the earth, where no one could see
them, the little white roots began to grow. They
grew longer and longer, down in the earth.
Most of them grew like ordinary turnips.

But right in the middle of the long, straight row, one little seed
grew *extra* long roots, longer and longer and LONGER.

Then little white shoots began to grow, up and up, and up
and up, until they came above the earth. And each little shoot
opened two green leaves to the sunshine. Most of them grew
like ordinary turnips. But right in the middle of the long,
straight row, one little shoot grew *extra* big leaves, bigger
and bigger and BIGGER.

" Look ! " said the little old man the grandfather.
" Come and look at the turnip seedlings."
    The little old woman the grandmother, the little girl
the grandchild, and the little black cat hurried down
the garden path. The little brown mouse came
from his secret place, and he ran down
the path as well.

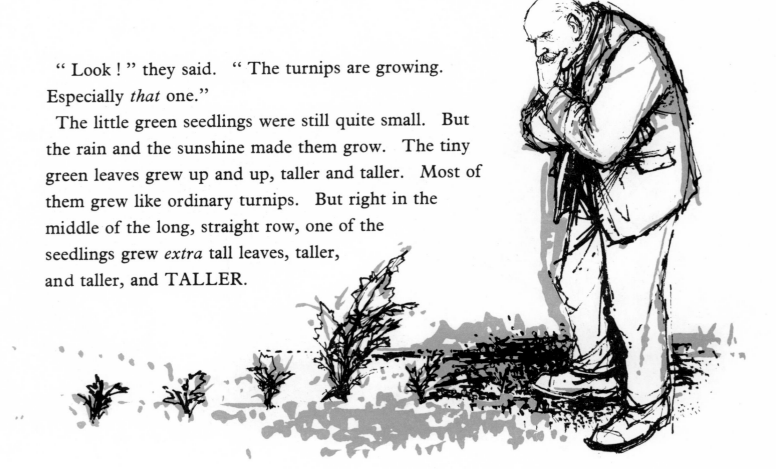

" Look ! " they said. " The turnips are growing. Especially *that* one."

The little green seedlings were still quite small. But the rain and the sunshine made them grow. The tiny green leaves grew up and up, taller and taller. Most of them grew like ordinary turnips. But right in the middle of the long, straight row, one of the seedlings grew *extra* tall leaves, taller, and taller, and TALLER.

Under the earth, where no one
could see them, round white turnips
began to grow. At first they were
very small indeed, but day by day,
and week by week, they grew and grew.
Most of them grew like ordinary turnips.
But right in the middle of the long,
straight row, one of them grew and
grew and GREW. It grew bigger and
bigger and BIGGER.

Above the earth, the leaves grew taller.
Beneath the earth, the turnips grew bigger.
Especially *that* one.   It grew bigger, and
bigger, and bigger, and BIGGER.
" It's ENORMOUS ! " said the
little old man the grandfather.

He stood and looked at the long straight row, and
he smiled. Then he said : " I shall pull a turnip out
of the ground, and we'll all have turnip soup for supper.
I shall pull up *that* one."

He went to the middle of the long straight row,
and took a firm hold of the turnip plant, the extra big,
ENORMOUS one.

Then he began to pull and pull.

He pulled, and he pulled, and he pulled.

But he *could* not pull up the turnip.

The little old man the grandfather called : " Little old woman the grandmother, please come and help me to pull up the turnip."

" Certainly," said the little old woman the grandmother.

She took a firm hold of the
little old man the grandfather's
waistcoat. And they pulled, and
they pulled, and they pulled.
But they *could* not pull up
the turnip.
The little old woman the
grandmother called : " Little
girl the grandchild, please
come and help us to
pull up the turnip."

" Certainly," said the little girl the grandchild.

She took a firm hold of the little old woman the grandmother's skirt.

And they pulled, and they pulled, and they pulled.

But they *could* not pull up the turnip.

The little girl the grandchild called :

"Little black cat, please come
and help us to pull up the turnip."

" Certainly," said the little black cat.
She took a firm hold of the little girl
the grandchild's apron strings. And they
pulled, and they pulled, and they pulled.
But they could *not* pull up the turnip.
What could they do?

The little black cat called :
" Little brown mouse, little brown
mouse, please come and help us to
pull up the turnip."
The little brown mouse came
from his secret place.
" Certainly," he said.
He took a firm hold of the black
cat's tail, and they pulled, and they
pulled, and they pulled.

And — UP came the turnip.

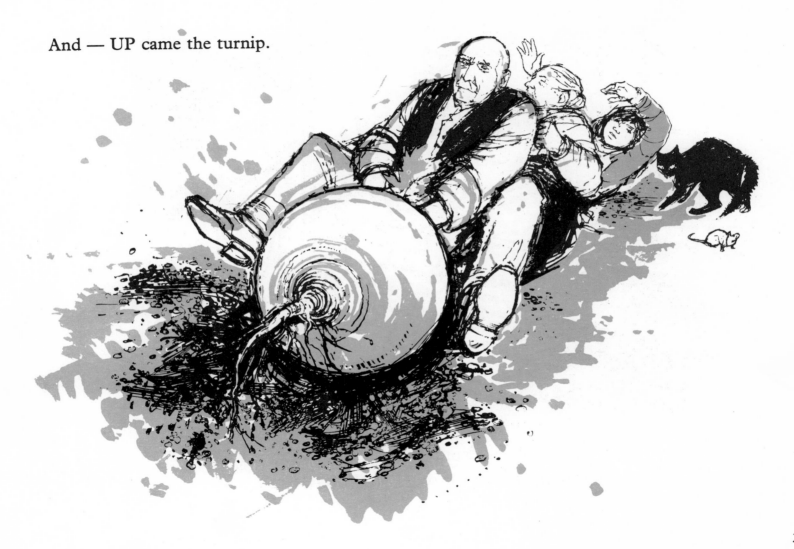

" There ! That's done," they said, and they carried
the turnip indoors. It was ENORMOUS.

It was so enormous that there was
enough for everybody.

There was enough for the little old man
the grandfather, and the little old woman
the grandmother, and the little girl the
grandchild, and the little black cat.

And the little brown mouse.